W9-AZZ-396

THE WOUNDED WOLF

THE WOUNDED WOLF

by *Jean Craighead George*

Pictures by *John Schoenherr*

Harper & Row, Publishers

New York, Hagerstown, San Francisco, London

J
Easy
George

FIRST EDITION

Library of Congress Cataloging in Publication Data
George, Jean Craighead, date
  The wounded wolf.

  SUMMARY: As hungry animals close in on an injured wolf, hoping to feed on him after death, help arrives.
  1. Wolves—Legends and stories. [1. Wolves—Fiction]
I. Schoenherr, John. II. Title.
PZ10.3.G316Wo 1978   [E]   76-58711
ISBN 0-06-021949-1
ISBN 0-06-021950-5 lib. bdg.

During his ten-year study of wolves in the Alaskan wilderness, scientist Gordon Haber, Ph.D., observed the leader of a wolf pack save the life of a wounded wolf.

A wounded wolf climbs Toklat Ridge,
a massive spine of rock and ice.
As he limps, dawn strikes the ridge
and lights it up with sparks and stars.
Roko, the wounded wolf, blinks in the ice fire,
then stops to rest and watch his pack
run the thawing Arctic valley.
They plunge and turn.
They fight the mighty caribou
that struck young Roko with his hoof
and wounded him.

He jumped between the beast and
Kiglo, leader of the Toklat pack.

Young Roko spun and fell.
Hooves, paws and teeth roared over him.
And then his pack and beast were gone.

Gravely injured, Roko pulls himself
toward the shelter rock.

Weakness overcomes him. He stops.
He and his pack are thin and hungry.
This is the season of starvation.
The winter's harvest has been taken.
The produce of spring has not begun.

Young Roko glances down the valley.
He droops his head and stiffens his tail
to signal to his pack
that he is badly hurt.

Winds wail.
A frigid blast picks up long shawls of snow
and drapes them between young Roko
and his pack.
And so his message is not read.

9

A raven scouting Toklat Ridge
sees Roko's signal.
"Kong, Kong, Kong," he bells—
death is coming to the Ridge;
there will be flesh and bone for all.

His voice rolls out across the valley.
It penetrates the rocky cracks
where the Toklat ravens rest.
One by one they hear and spread their wings.
They beat their way to Toklat Ridge.

They alight upon the snow
and walk behind the wounded wolf.
"Kong," they toll with keen excitement
for the raven clan is hungry, too.
"Kong, Kong"—
there will be flesh and bone for all.

Roko snarls
and hurries toward the shelter rock.

A cloud of snow envelopes him.
He limps in blinding whiteness now.
A ghostly presence flits around.

"Hahahahahahaha," the white fox states—
death is coming to the Ridge.
Roko smells the fox tagging at his heels.

The cloud whirls off.
Two golden eyes look up at Roko.
The snowy owl has heard the ravens
and joined the deathwatch.

13

Roko limps along.
The ravens walk.
The white fox leaps.
The snowy owl flies and hops
along the rim of Toklat Ridge.

Roko stops.
Below the ledge out on the flats
the musk-ox herd is circling.
They form a ring and all face out,
a fort of heads and horns
and fur that sweeps down to their hooves.
Their circle means to Roko that
an enemy is present.

He squints and smells the wind.

It carries scents of thawing ice,
broken grass—and earth.
The grizzly bear is up!
He has awakened from his winter's sleep.
A craving need for flesh will drive him.

Roko sees the shelter rock.
He strains to reach it.

He stumbles.
The ravens move in closer.
The white fox boldly walks beside him.
"Hahaha," he yaps.
The snowy owl flies ahead, alights and waits.

The grizzly hears the eager fox
and rises on his flat hind feet.
He twists his powerful neck and head.
His great paws dangle at his chest.

He sees the animal procession
and hears the ravens' knell of death.
Dropping to all fours
he joins the march up Toklat Ridge.

Roko stops, his breath comes hard.
A raven alights upon his back
and picks the open wound.
Roko snaps. The raven flies
and circles back.
The white fox nips at Roko's toes.
The snowy owl inches closer.

The grizzly bear, still dulled by sleep,
stumbles onto Toklat Ridge.

Only yards from the shelter rock,
Roko falls.

Instantly the ravens mob him.
They scream and peck and stab his eyes.
The white fox leaps upon his wound.
The snowy owl sits and waits.

Young Roko struggles to his feet.
He bites the ravens.
Snaps the fox.
And lunges at the stoic owl.
He turns and warns the grizzly bear.
Then he bursts into a run
and falls against the shelter rock.

The wounded wolf wedges down
between the rock and barren ground.
Now protected on three sides
he turns and faces all his foes.

The ravens step a few feet closer.
The fox slides toward him on his belly.
The snowy owl blinks and waits,
and on the Ridge rim
roars the hungry grizzly bear.

Roko growls.

The sun comes up.
Far across the Toklat Valley
Roko hears his pack's "hunt's end" song.
The music wails and sobs,
wilder than the bleating wind.

The hunt song ends.
Next comes the roll call.
Each member of the Toklat pack barks
to say that he is home and well.
"Kiglo here," Roko hears his leader bark.
There is a pause. It is young Roko's turn.
He cannot lift his head to answer.

The pack is silent.
The leader starts the count once more.
"Kiglo here."
—A pause.
Roko cannot answer.

The wounded wolf whimpers softly.
A mindful raven hears.
"KONG, KONG, KONG," he tolls
—this is the end.

His booming sounds across the valley.
The wolf pack hears the raven's message
that something is dying.
They know it is Roko
who has not answered roll call.

The hours pass.
The wind slams snow on Toklat Ridge.
Massive clouds blot out the sun.
In their gloom Roko sees
the deathwatch move in closer.

Suddenly he hears the musk-oxen
thundering into their circle.
The ice cracks as the grizzly leaves.
The ravens burst into the air.
The white fox runs.
The snowy owl flaps to the top of the shelter rock

and Kiglo rounds the knoll.

In his mouth he carries meat.
He drops it close to Roko's head
and wags his tail excitedly.
Roko licks Kiglo's chin to honor him.
Then Kiglo puts his mouth around Roko's nose.
This gesture says "I am your leader."
And by mouthing Roko he binds him
and all the wolves together.

The wounded wolf wags his tail.
Kiglo trots away.

Already Roko's wound feels better.
He gulps the food
and feels his strength return.

He shatters bone, flesh and gristle
and shakes the scraps out on the snow.

The hungry ravens swoop upon them.
The white fox snatches up a bone.
The snowy owl gulps down flesh and fur.
And Roko wags his tail and watches.

For days Kiglo brings young Roko food.
He gnashes, gorges and shatters bits upon the snow.

A purple sandpiper winging north
sees ravens, owl and fox.
And he drops in upon the feast.

The long-tailed jaeger gull flies down
and joins the crowd on Toklat Ridge.

Roko wags his tail.

One dawn he moves his wounded leg. He stretches it
and pulls himself into the sunlight.
He walks—he romps. He runs in circles.
He leaps and plays with chunks of ice.
Suddenly he stops.
The "hunt's end" song rings out.

Next comes the roll call.
"Kiglo here."
"Roko here," he barks out strongly.
The pack is silent.
"Kiglo here," the leader repeats.
"Roko here."

Across the distance comes the sound
of whoops and yipes and barks and howls.
They fill the dawn with celebration.

And Roko prances down the Ridge.